For my sister Pam, with love
~ P. B.

For Ravi, Patrycja and
Mehrdad, with love ~ B. C.

Text copyright © Paul Bright 2006
Illustrations copyright © Ben Cort 2006

Original edition published in English by Little Tiger Press,
an imprint of Magi Publications, London, England, 2006.

Printed in Singapore by Tien Wah Press Pte.

Library of Congress Cataloging-in-Publication Data

Bright, Paul.
I'm not going out there! / Paul Bright ; [illustrated by] Ben Cort.
p. cm.
Summary: Monsters, witches, and even a dragon quake in fear
when a prank transforms an ordinary person into a terrible beast.
ISBN-13: 978-1-56148-535-2 (hardcover : alk. paper)
[1. Monsters--Fiction. 2. Fear--Fiction. 3. Brothers and sisters--Fiction.
4. Humorous stories. 5. Stories in rhyme.]   I. Title: I am not going out there!.
II. Cort, Ben, ill. III. Title.

PZ8.3.B7675Iam 2006
[E]--dc22
2006003098

Paul Bright   Ben Cort

I'm Not Going Out There!

Good Books

Intercourse, PA 17534
800/762-7171
www.GoodBks.com

I am underneath the bed,
Hardly poking out my head.
It's a squeeze and hurts my knees,
but I don't really care.
Can you guess, do you know,
Why I whisper soft and low?

I'M

NOT

GOING

OUT

THERE!

There's a dragon breathing smoke,
Who looks far too fierce to stroke,
And his eyes have got a scary sort of stare.
I hope he doesn't stay,
But he's not what makes me say,

I'M NOT GOING OUT THERE!

There's a ghost who's got no head,
With some toast and chocolate spread
Which I'm sure he would be very
pleased to share.
And even though I'd like a bite,
Still I'm keeping out of sight.

I'M NOT GOING OUT THERE!

There are witches, old and stubbly,
'Round a bath all hot and bubbly,
Busy washing all their dirty underwear,
Hanging knickers out to dry,
But they're not the reason why

I'M NOT GOING OUT THERE!

There are monsters of all sizes,
Doing dancing exercises,
Wearing tutus, with pink ribbons in their hair.
And even though they look quite charming,
There is something else alarming;

I'M NOT GOING

Suddenly there's a shrieking—
And a squealing and a squeaking,
Loud enough to give the boldest beast
a scare.
Now I'm shaking and I'm quaking—
There's a noise of something breaking.

I'M NOT GOING OUT THERE!

The dragon turns quite pale,
From his nostrils to his tail.
While his dragon heart starts pounding,
Up the stairs he's flapping, bounding.
"Mustn't panic!" gasps the ghost.
"Keep your head! Don't lose your toast!
I can haunt some other day,
Now I need to get away!"

All the witches spill their washing
And go splishing, splashing, sploshing,
Screeching spells to get things dried,
And to find a place to hide.
Hide from what? They'll soon find out!
They can hear it scream and shout.
Better hurry! Better run!
'Cause it doesn't sound like fun.

Even the monsters don't feel brave,
'Though they try hard to behave,
So they dance off in a row,
Each one on his tippy-toe.

Then all that I can hear,
Very loud and very near,
Is the thing that made them flee.
Do you know what it could be?

It's got teeth that bite and gnash;
It's got eyes that dart and flash.
We can hear it grumping, jumping,
Hear it stamping, stomping, thumping.
It's got hands that pinch and snatch;
It's got nails that claw and scratch.
It sounds ready for a fight;
We squeeze in and squash up tight!

There it is—my sister Kate!
And she's in a frightful state,
Making shrieking sounds,
and leaping in the air.
For, you see, she now knows who
Put the spider in her shoe!

I'M NOT GOING OUT THERE!